To my grandsons: Nolan, Leland, and Emmett. May you always have
great adventures, and never get caught.

R.B.

All my love to my wonderful husband, who made this book possible.

L.J.M.

Summary: In this work of fiction a mischievous mouse is hastily pursued by family members, staff and assorted guests in a hilarious romp through the most famous residence in the United States of America.

[1. White House 2. Mouse 3. First Family 4. Rose Garden 5.Washington 6. Chase]

ISBN-13: 978-1-945518-00-3
ISBN-10: 1945518-00-6

Printed in the U.S.A.

A Mouse in the White House

by Richard Ballo

Illustrated by Lisa J. Michaels

THIS is The White House in Washington, DC.

THIS is a.... *mouse*

"There's a MOUSE in the White House!" yelled the First Kid.

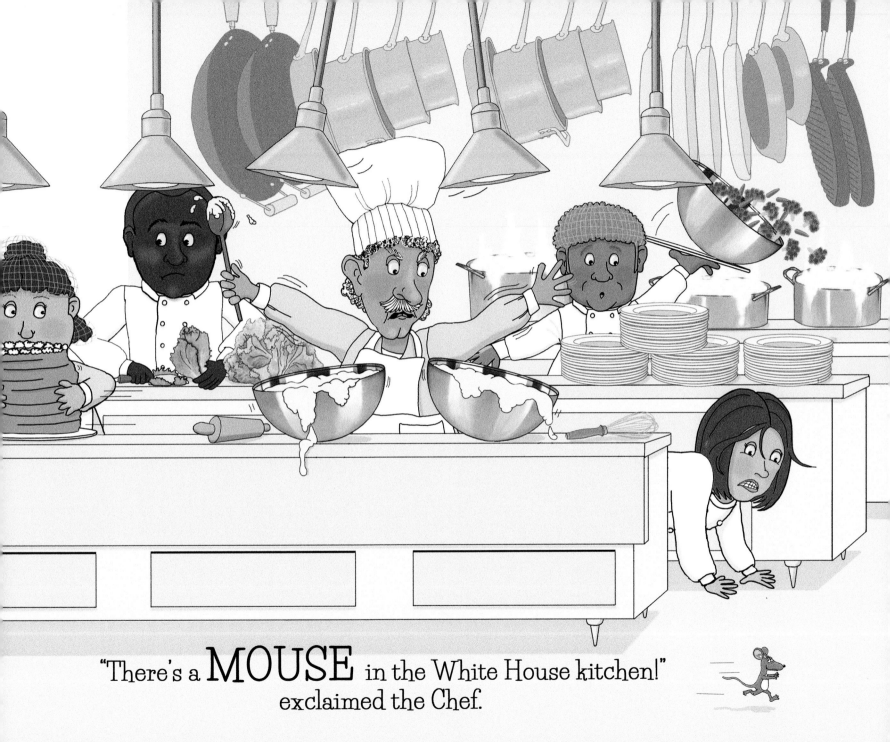

"There's a MOUSE in the White House kitchen!" exclaimed the Chef.

"I'll catch him," cried the First Kid.
"Get out of here!" demanded the Chef.

"There's a mouse in the White House," whispered the Secret Service Agent.

"I'll catch him," repeated the First Kid.
"Let me at him," shrieked the Chef.
"I have him in my sight, repeat...
I have the mouse in sight,"
whispered the Agent.

"You're mine now, little mouse!" said the Chef.

He's headed for the Oval Office," whispered the Agent, "inform the President."

"Can I ask a few questions?"
shouted the Reporter.

"There's a mouse in the White House," shrieked the First Lady.

"He's slipping away!"
the First Kid howled.

"He won't get away
from ME," the Chef
bellowed.

"...Repeat, the mouse is escaping!" whispered the Agent.

"This is the house of the PEOPLE!" exclaimed the First Lady.

"Is that a MOUSE in my
White House?" asked the President.

"Oui," said the French Ambassador.

Hiss-s-s...

Jack, the Presidents' cat, waited in the hallway.

"Get him!" the First Kid charged ahead.
"He must not get away," the Chef proclaimed.
"Stand down...I repeat, STAND DOWN," said the Agent.
"This'll make a GREAT story!" the Reporter grinned.

"Where's the Vice President when you need him?" shouted the First Lady.

"Oui, Oui," agreed the French Ambassador.

"Where's pest control when you need them?" asked the President.

Jack, the cat, imagined a mousy dinner.

The mouse ran through the French doors...

...and into the Rose Garden.

Everyone sighed.
Jack growled.
"How will we get him out of there?"
asked the Gardener.

"Why get him out?" asked the First Kid.

Everyone turned and went back inside...

...and so did the mouse.